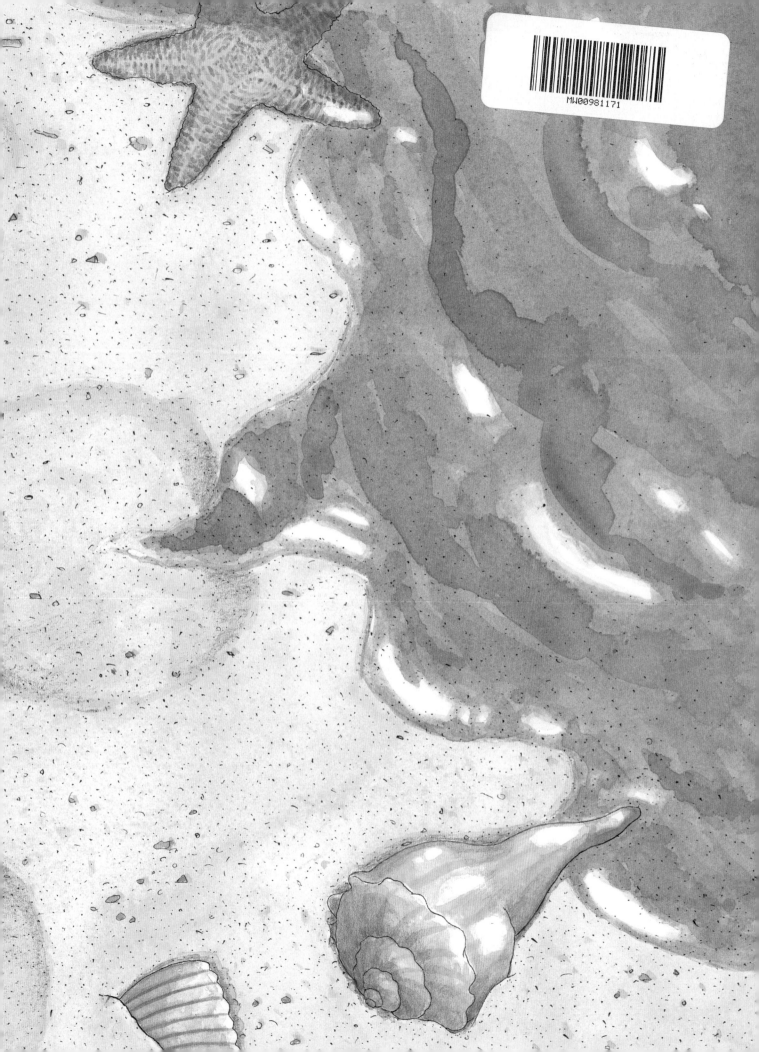

THE HIPPOS AT THE SEASHORE

❖❖Lindsay Grater❖❖

LESTER PUBLISHING LIMITED

CANADIAN CATALOGUING IN PUBLICATION DATA

Grater, Lindsay, 1952-
The hippos at the seashore

ISBN 1-895555-25-6

I. Title.

PS8563.R3H56 1993   jC813'.54   C92-095474-X
PZ7.G73Hip 1993

Lester Publishing Limited
56 The Esplanade
Toronto, Ontario
Canada M5E 1A7

Printed and bound in Hong Kong

93 94 95 96 5 4 3 2 1

Thinking of Nina

"**W**e're here, everyone!" shouted Father Hippo, pointing down to the beach. "That must be the cottage."

"Oh dear, it looks very small," murmured Mother Hippo.

"Don't worry, Lily," said Granny. "It will be fine."

"Beat you into the sea, Rollo!" they heard Rosie yell from the beach.

"I was right," said Mother. "It *is* tiny. And look at this dust everywhere!"

"You can see daylight through the roof," added Father. "I'm afraid you won't be very comfortable here, Granny."

"I'll manage," Granny replied. "Now, let's go and join the children."

The Hippos had been planning their holiday activities for weeks.

Rollo built a sturdy sandcastle.

Rosie collected delicate shells.

Father exercised and Mother painted.

Late in the afternoon, Granny peered out to sea.

"There are some nasty storm clouds blowing this way," she warned the others.

A chilly breeze sprang up. Cold drops of rain plopped on the sand.

"Quickly – gather everything up and run indoors!" Mother called.

"What about my sandcastle?" wailed Rollo.

"I'll help you build an even better one tomorrow," Rosie offered kindly.

It was impossible to stay warm and dry in the flimsy cottage. At bedtime the storm was still howling. Only Granny managed to get some sleep.

"I have lived through worse storms than this," she muttered. Then she rolled over and began to snore.

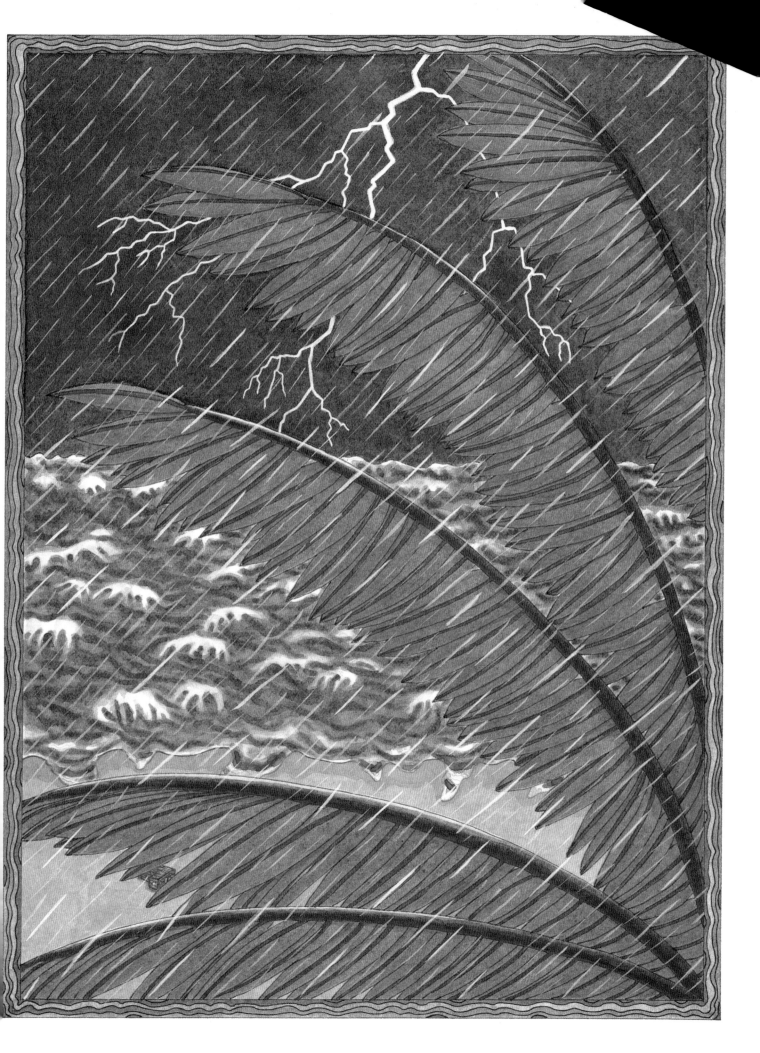

In the morning Granny made breakfast for her tired and irritable family. Rosie shouted at Rollo when he spilled some mashed banana on her sweater. Then Rollo remembered that Rosie had left his new pail and shovel outside when the rain started. He began to cry.

"Surely this storm can't carry on much longer," Mother sighed.

But the storm did carry on.

It was a very small cottage to hold five hippos. Tempers wore thin. Things came to a head when the gusting wind smashed through a window.

"This place is just a tumbledown shack!" bellowed Father.

"We're all going to catch pneumonia!" roared Mother.

"My holiday is completely ruined!" sobbed Rosie.

"My beautiful sandcastle is ruined too," cried Rollo, "and I can't build another one because Rosie has lost my pail and shovel!"

"Calm down!" Granny said firmly. "Getting angry does not help. Do something useful!"

Mother blocked up the window with her drawing-board.

Father picked up a piece of the broken window frame. He hammered at the loose nails in the roof.

Rosie and Rollo found sticky tape and glue in their mother's art supply box to plug the holes in the walls.

"Now, that's better," commented Granny as she swept up the broken glass.

As the cottage became cosy the Hippos cheered up.

"If I can't exercise outside, I'll exercise inside," said Father.

"If I can't paint a calm sea, I'll paint a rough one," said Mother.

"If I can't collect shells, I'll read about them," said Rosie.

"If I can't make a sandcastle, I'll draw one," said Rollo.

"I can hear the rain stopping," Granny said that evening. "We shall see the sun tomorrow."

The Hippos could not resist running out in the moonlight to stretch their legs.

"Look what I found, Rollo!" called Rosie as she pulled his pail and shovel from under a rock.

Brilliant morning sunshine woke the Hippos. They watched the sun warm the beach while they ate their breakfast.

They ran to the beach, determined to make up for lost time. Nothing was going to spoil their fun.

At the end of a busy day, the Hippos enjoyed a picnic supper.

Father turned to Granny. "You've been wonderful on this holiday. We could not have coped without you."

"Well," answered Granny, "you can't let a few drops of rain get you down."

"By the way," Mother asked, "what have you been knitting all week?"

"A special blanket," Granny chuckled. "One that will always remind us of this holiday. There," she added as she cut the yarn, "it's all finished!"

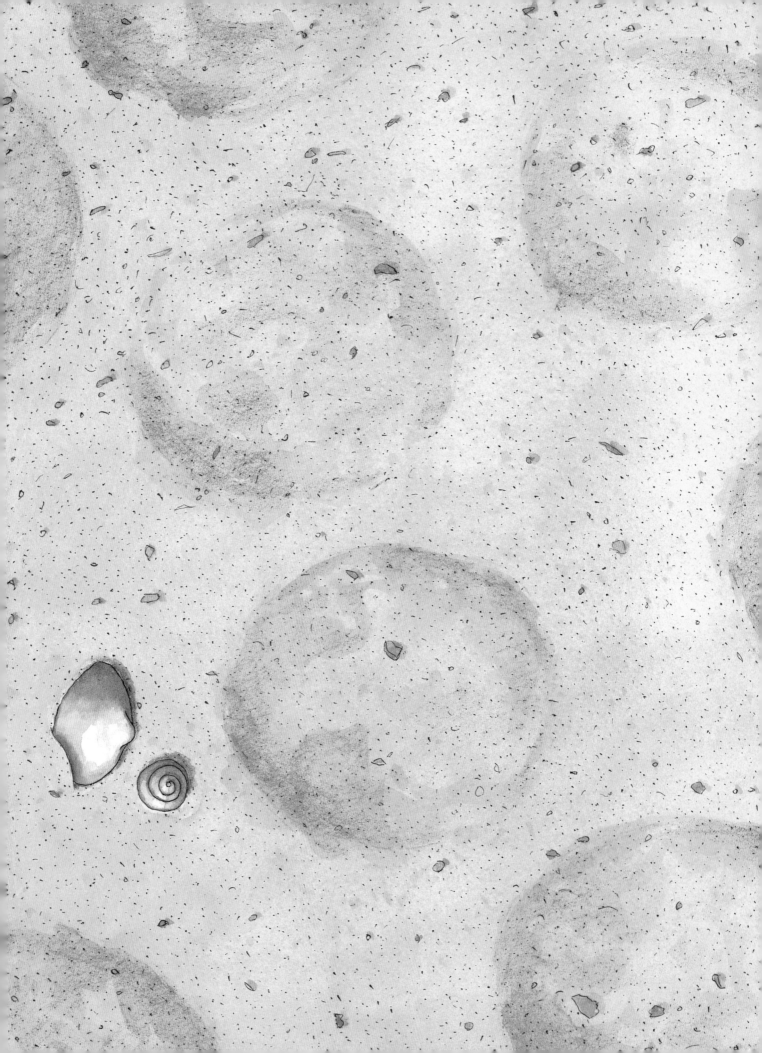